D1571668

To request permission, contact the author at
start@poweringempathy.com

Hardcover: ISBN# 9780578696935
eBook: ISBN# 9781737467205
Library of Congress Number: 2021912469
Cover art by: Joleen Sheldon
                    Kamilla Kiil Egballe Heinze
Interior art by: Joleen Sheldon
                    Kamilla Kiil Egballe Heinze

www.emotionaltheater.com
www.poweringempathy.com

There once was a forest so gray
all those who emerged felt dismay.
They left feeling bad,
quite somber and sad,
and wondered what ruined their day.

The source of the forest's sadness,
such total darkness and drabness,

was found in the frown
just south of the crown
on the forest's Royal Highness.

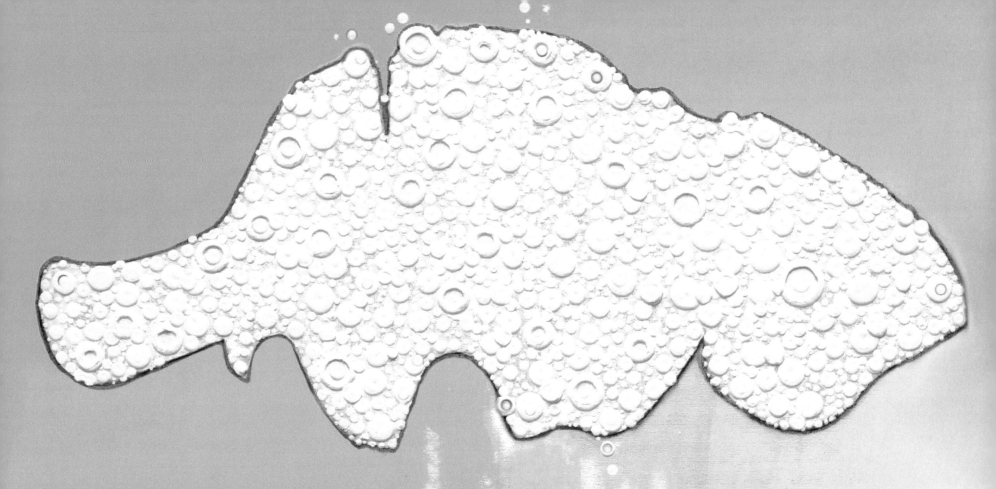

She wore that frown morning till night.
There it stayed by only moonlight.
The forest grew dim.
The future looked grim,

not a glimmer of hope in sight.

Weary of the queen's somber rule,
her frown as stubborn as a mule,
the forest began
to form its own plan
to find a hilarious fool.

Scrolled on a leaf, the message read,
"Joy fast! Can't last!" That's all it said.
The winds blew up strong.
The leaf flew along
and carried the message ahead.

That leaf floated down from the air
and landed in the springy hair
of a world class jester.
"Please do call me Lester.
I'm known to spread joy on a dare."

"At most it will take me three tries.
Of that I can safely surmise.
If she doesn't smile
in just a short while,
I'll head down the road with no prize."

Off to the queen they did hurry,
the jester without a worry,
and that's when he spoke
a very old joke
she'd surely have to find worthy.

"How's gum cross the road unflicken?"
asked Lester. His voice did quicken.

The queen slowly sighed,
and then she replied,
"Stuck to the foot of that chicken."

"Did you think I was on the hook?
That's the oldest joke in the book!
If that was your best,
you can skip the rest."

But Lester refused to be shook.

He launched into his second act,
a jig that was more action-packed,
a dance filled with danger
that kept getting stranger,
but her frown stayed firmly intact.

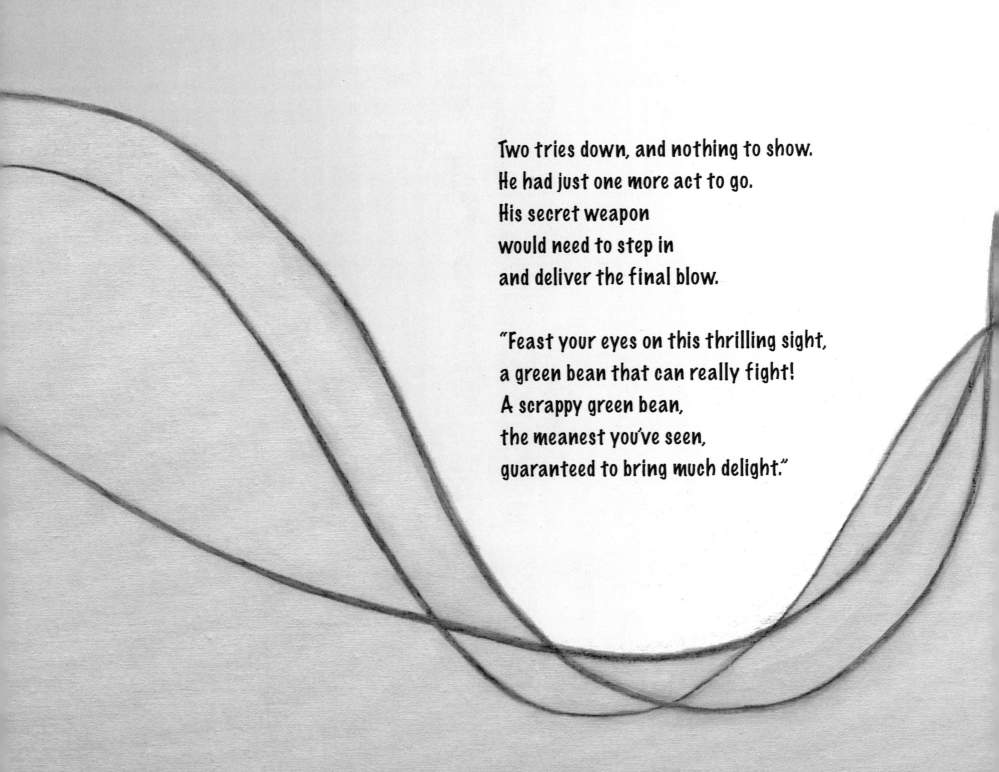

Two tries down, and nothing to show.
He had just one more act to go.
His secret weapon
would need to step in
and deliver the final blow.

"Feast your eyes on this thrilling sight,
a green bean that can really fight!
A scrappy green bean,
the meanest you've seen,
guaranteed to bring much delight."

The bean and Lester huddled near,
then Lester whispered in his ear.
The forest waited,
quite captivated.
What would happen next was unclear.

The bean's face lit up like a flare.
He cartwheeled into Lester's hair,

messed up the strange do
with stylish kung fu
and left it in great disrepair.

Page 21 Anger

A slide down the bridge of the nose,
and there's where he stood in crane pose.

Eye to eye they stared.
"Don't blink!" the bean dared,
then Lester's lids began to close.

The bean's next attack snuck up fast,
not even a second had passed.
Without any class,
he let out some gas
as Lester jumped back from the blast!

The queen watched with perplexed delight.
That bean really put up a fight.
Her frown disappeared.
Her face felt so weird,
and oddly she felt less uptight.

Feelings long since forgotten were stirred,
then something amazing occurred.
Where her frown had been,
there emerged a grin
from watching a fight so absurd.

Her grin remained only awhile
before growing into a smile.
Soon laughter burst out
and echoed throughout
the leaves of the trees for a mile.

The forest then shouted out loud,
"Laughter is finally allowed!
Let us celebrate!
That jester was great!"
Then Lester stood up, and he bowed.

"I really must know," said the queen,
"what riled up your feisty green bean?
What was it you said
that got in his head
and made him so ornery and mean?"

"I told him of your stubborn frown.
He knows what it's like to feel down.
We then staged that fight
in hopes that it might
bring a smile to turn things around."

The forest was feeling revived.
Lester and the green bean high-fived.
"We did it!" they said.
"We got smiles to spread.
Good times have finally arrived!"

The queen laughed and laughed with delight.
More jubilant days were in sight.
The forest was free
to revel in glee.
The future looked happy and bright.

THE END

The fun has just begun!
Head to the Emotional
Theater and join the
cast backstage as they
rehearse their emotions!

VISIT US!

EMOTIONALTHEATER.COM

ABOUT THE AUTHOR

Joleen Sheldon

Joleen Sheldon is the author, artist, and illustrator of *Jester Lester And The Mean Green Bean*. A visual artist for more than 25 years, her striking artwork has been featured in galleries from Chicago to the Rocky Mountains.

Joleen has also written a chapter book titled *The Emotional Theater Talent Show*, and created an interactive website at emotionaltheater.com

EMOTIONAL THEATER

WHERE EMOTIONS TAKE CENTER STAGE

emotionaltheater.com

OTHER

by Joleen Sheldon

BOOKS

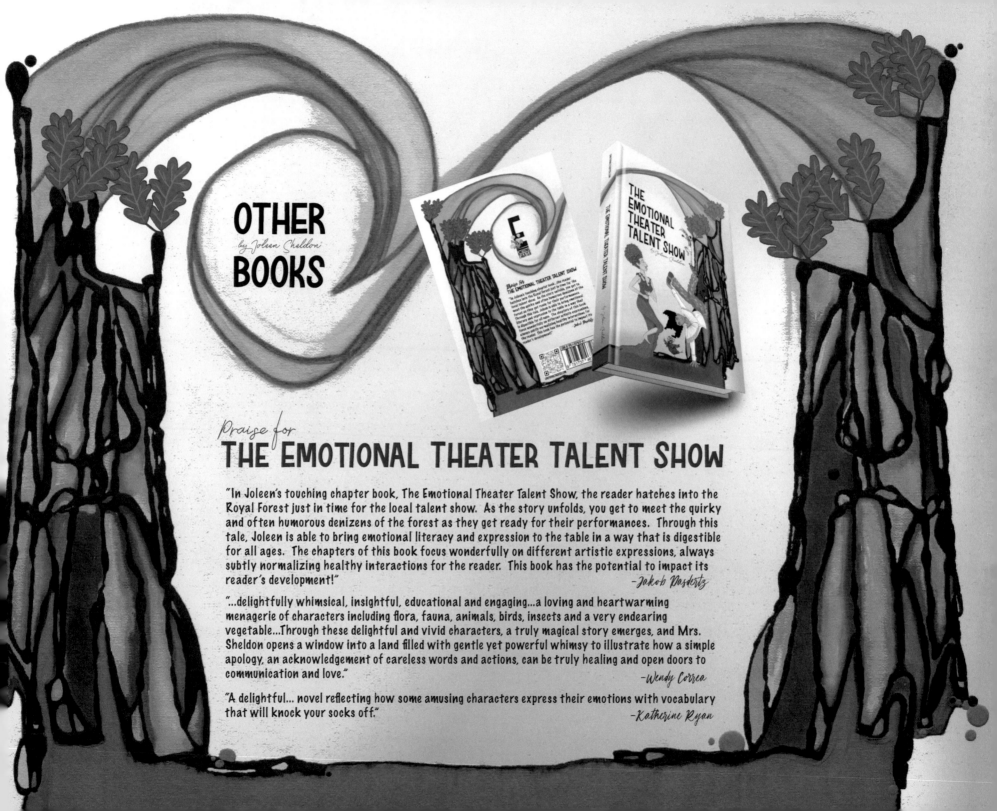

LEARN MORE!

POWERINGEMPATHY.COM

We Believe
EDUCATION+EMOTIONAL INTELLIGENCE+ACTIVE PARTICIPATION=CHANGE
Visit www.poweringempathy.com Today!

CPSIA information can be obtained
at www.ICGtesting.com
Printed in the USA
BVRC100831210921
617186BV00008B/290